Happy
Birthday
to Sera!

I could think
of no
better gift
in the world
than this.

— Jonnie L
LTK 2/27/08

CONTENT:

Selected Blog Posts from Jonnie 7-11

By Jonnie Gilliom

Recipient of Gooseneck's

Golden Goose Award of Excellence

Printed by LuLu

ISBN: 978-1-4116-9179-7

To purchase additional copies:

http://www.lulu.com/jonnie711

•

Jonnie 7-11

Dedication

To my Liebling, Sandra Thum (a.k.a. Black Bettie).

Du bist sehr hübsch und Ich bin hart wie Krupp-stahl.

Meeting Sandralein was easily the best thing to come out of my blogging experience.

Acknowledgements

After Sandralein[1], I would also thank Boz[2] for the inspiration to blog in the first place, for being an Internet Icon, and for mailing me Faygo Redpop from the Midwest. Also, thanks to AmyJo[3] for writing this book's *Introduction*, for proof reading the manuscript, and for inventing the name *Rebel Leady Boy* (which is *Labor Ready Boy* pronounced with a Japanese accent). ~~Also Belle[4] for being a role model~~, Purple Viper[5] for the Nixon showerhead, The Umpire (Gooseneck - the greatest living Iowan)[6], JohnnyC[7] for his raw enthusiasm, *The Real World…Blogger Style*[8] for providing a virtual hangout, Labor Ready for quick cash, the Amish, the Gilliom family, Donald "Another Mother" Kilbuck, my lawyer Jon David, and all the other bloggers who have contributed commentary over the years.

[1] http://blackbettie.blogspot.com

[2] http://nomoreboz.blogpot.com

[3] http://stoneandstar.blogspot.com

[4] http://asortakindafairytale.blogspot.com/

[5] http://purpleviper.blogspot.com/

[6] http://behindtheplate.blogspot.com

[7] http://juanbodley.blogspot.com

[8] http://realworldbloggerstyle.blogspot.com

About Jonnie 7-11

Jonnie Gilliom (a.k.a. Jonnie 7-11, a.k.a. Nacho Steppinstone, a.k.a. Rebel Leady Boy) spent his formative years in Northeastern Indiana's Amish country until wandering to Alaska where he remained throughout most of the 1990s.

By 2000, Jonnie had relocated to the continental USA's west coast and currently resides in Orange County, California where he recently completed a Master's program in Information Science. He finds it humorous that his diploma bears the signature of California Governor, Arnold Schwarzenegger. Jonnie is currently preoccupied with bringing his fiancée, Sandra, over from Germany and then will be preoccupied with trying to obtain professional employment as an archivist.

Jonnie's original blog, *I'm Nacho Steppinstone*, was retired in May, 2005. He currently blogs as *Rebel Leady Boy*[1] and is an active contributor to *The Real World…Blogger Style!*[2] and *Jonnie & Boz's 99 Cent Blog*[3].

[1] http://pancakepancake.blogspot.com

[2] http://realworldbloggerstyle.blogspot.com

[3] http://the99centstoreblog.blogspot.com

Contents

Like Mayflies On A Summer Night: Ephemera and the Hardcore by AmyJo 17

Furthermore by Donald Kilbuck 21

Foreward by Jonnie 7-11 23

I. Cheap Thrills 25

      Shaving Cream Head 27

      Fork Fangs 29

      Hit 'Em Again 31

      Dashboard Dough 32

      Boing! 33

      One Dollar 34

      Dictionary + Fire Game 35

      Putt-Putt 36

      Jello Sticks 38

      Plaster 38

      Grapette Memories 40

II. Youthful Folly 43

      Retarded Moments 45

      Action Men 46

      Amish Roots 46

      Solomon W. 47

Time Capsule 47

1984 Revisited 49

Selected Journal Entries 50

Seven Stupid Dreams 51

Momentum 52

Pinewood Derby 53

III. Autobiographical Accounts 55

P-E-P-S-I S-P-R-I-T 57

Chili Dog Burrito 58

Burrito Freakout 59

A Whole Different Sandwich 61

Broke Down 61

Hyderization 63

First Impressions. 65

4th Avenue 66

California, Here We Come 67

Learning Stick 69

Hit By A Train 71

Office Party 73

Jonnie Homemaker 74

Central Air 74

Labor Ready Revisited 75

Coyotes in These Here Hills 77

Pantsless in the OC 78

IV. Interpersonal 79

Sandra In L.A: "Oh My God! Look At All the Trucks!" 81

99 Cent Anecdote 83

Traveling Exhibit 84

Jay, the Former Carnie 86

Knecht Ruprecht 89

Unsung Heroes 91

Crisis Line 91

Three Cool Things About My Mechanic 92

Black Carlos Was Right 93

True Security Guard Fantasies 94

V. Introducing: Donald Kilbuck, Soul Saver .97

Introduction 99

Xmas Cheer – For Free! 100

Kilbuckian Prophecy 101

Porcupine Quills 101

From Another Mother 102

When a Bear Awakes, What It Means to Hikers! 106

DK on Unsavory Characters 107

VI. Good Ideas 109

    Testing 111

    Toad Licking 111

    Publicity Stunt 112

    Schizo Coffee 112

    Tattoo Idea 113

    Glue-All 114

    RLB's Time Saving Tips 115

    Perpetual Motion 116

    Soul Food 116

    What Do You Want? 117

VII. Souvenirs and Ephemera 119

    Paging Mick Ulmer, Oriental Guide 121

    Taco Bell Scrapbook 123

    On the Floor 123

    The Muse Was Here 125

    Thou Shalt Not Croak 126

    FYI 128

    Something You Don't See Everyday 129

    A Place to Store My Hulk Hands 130

From Jonnie's Utility Belt. 131

My Linguistic Profile 132

Ephemera Deluxe 133

From PVC 134

Self-Knowledge 135

An After-word by Jon David 137

Like Mayflies on a Summer Night: Ephemera and the Hardcore

Jonnie, an introduction

by AmyJo

Ephemera:

1: something transitory; lasting a day

2: an insect that lives only for a day in its winged form, i.e. a mayfly

3: A short-lived thing.

4: Printed matter of passing interest.

Hardcore:

1. a form of music with hard fast delivery.

simple and effective sounds, mainly focussed [sic] on a message. message is ussually [sic] unity, anarky, [sic] strength or public power.

2. **HARDCORE** is the limit, it is the core of cool things! It is the mother of things!

(1 &2. source, the Urban Dictionary)

hard-core also **hard core** (härd'kôr', -kōr')
adj.

1. Intensely loyal; die-hard: *a hard-core secessionist; a hard-core golfer.*
2. Stubbornly resistant to improvement or change: *hard-core poverty.*
3. Extremely graphic or explicit: *hard-core pornography.*

In the pages that follow we see what happens when an archivist with absurdist tendencies catalogues the minutiae of daily existence. But Jonnie is no nebbish, collecting facts and sticking them like boogers to the page. Here are no dull recitations of the collector, no dry scraps preserved in a vacuum. Rather we find a compendium at once familiar and revelatory—incidents, memories, processes, encounters—that reveal the texture both of everyday life, and the mind of their chronicler—a texture that is not unlike the orange dust that clings to your fingers after eating a bag of Cheetos—sticky, flavorful, impossible to get out from under your nails.

In Jonnie 7-11's book you will discover the intersection of the ephemeral and the hardcore. One might assume that these two qualities are contradictory, but in Jonnie's work the paradox reveals a space where life itself is illuminated with uncommon intensity.

There is no doubt that Jonnie is hardcore. From early childhood to his fully-fledged manhood, Jonnie has exhibited the balls-to-the-wall willingness to explore the world as it is and to interact with what's right there in front of him. Whether he is breaking rocks for eight hours a day , practicing mole removal with ordinary nail clippers, conducting experiments by micturating into his own visage, chasing Amish buggies or freight trains, encountering day laborers, his Liebling, archivists, bloggers, landlords, esquimaux, drunks, golfers or schizophrenics, Jonnie does not shrink from experience. No subject, no matter how mundane, no person, no matter how crazy, escapes his notice. As Jonnie himself professes, he has an affection for stupidity.

At first glance this book might seem like a compendium of ephemera— disconnected and utterly without point. Jonnie himself calls his blog (from which these entries were drawn) "a place to store my stuff". However, taken all together, what emerges in these pages is, for me at least, truly rare. Behind the fork fangs and the hulk hands and the pirate salute is a person who strikes me as kind and intelligent and imaginative and wise.

Read between the lines of his anecdotes and the ephemera he presents will remind you that life—fleeting, ordinary life—can be exciting and fun. This is a powerful thing to do. On the surface his anecdotes and craft projects are hilarious—but after continued exposure they become— absurdly-- uplifting.

Jonnie first came to me by reputation, as the librettist and chief tenor of his dadaist masterpiece, The Toilet Opera. His aria "hear my flush, fear my flush", even at secondhand, is unforgettable. On the basis of that single exuberant couplet, I concluded that Jonnie Gilliom was a man whose hand I'd be proud to shake (after we both washed, of course).

Nearly ten years later, Boz, Jonnie and I gathered online and audio-blogged excerpts from "Bat Out of Hell". I was grieving the suicide of a dear friend and laid up in bed with a broken ankle. My family were all far away. So were my friends. But online, the three of us had what I will always consider a wake. Jonnie didn't speak any traditional words of sympathy. Sentimentality isn't his style. But he sang Meatloaf into a pillow while wearing a Frankenstein mask, baying into the phone in his signature tuneless Frank Zappa voice and , four hundred miles away, I laughed until I cried.

I don't know if he even remembers that night, and it doesn't matter. At a time when I couldn't be consoled, that evening—three dorks screaming songs into the phone and zonking about Meatloaf—helped me get through a really bad night. To me, that is Jonnie. I don't know how he does it, but he makes me feel that life is good.

I have been following Jonnie's work on the web for almost three years now, and over the course of that time his writing has captivated me, instructed me, comforted me, and won my respect.

So settle in. Let Jonnie teach you the deeper meaning of what it is to be hardcore. Embrace the ephemeral with courage and humor. Let this book remind you that, somewhere out there in the flickering light of the Del Taco sign, under the swaying palm trees of the OC, a man with a vision cares enough to write about those ephemeral moments that are born and pass away like mayflies on a summer night—brief, beautiful, pointless, and profound.

Furthermore

By Donald Kilbuck

The Introduction for the book! Real or reel! You may feel this introduction for all the feelings that people have, has, fast, faster, motions may feel motionless, butt the earth may swallow you up if you're not all there. The stink of whatever, if you wear it. Although i got the tide, tightrobe, out into this Island and feel the changing weather, and the emotions may catch all your feelings, vomit isn't all what it seems. Getting a speeding ticket also.

Foreward

By Jonnie 7-11

Rebel Leady Boy is a practical & earthy Virgo. I'm using this blog as a scrapbook & diary of everyday life. Expect no lofty platitudes here. This is not a writing exercise. It's a place to store my stuff. Feel free to rummage through, you might find something useful among all the crap.

- Rebel Leady Boy's Mission Statement

The title of this book is "**con**tent", as in "web content"; rather than "con**tent**", as in "I am quite content". I hope it isn't mistaken for a self-help book. And, yes, I think it's funny to give my book a confusing and/or potentially misleading title.

This book recreates selected blog posts for my own amusement and from a lack of faith in the long-term reliability of digital media. When you really want to keep a copy of something, it's best to print it on ink and paper. I occasionally included comments from other bloggers when they enhanced the discussion at hand. I also thought this was a good opportunity to introduce Donald Kilbuck to the world.

If you enjoy this book, donate a copy to your local library.

Jonnie with Hulk Hands.

Cheap Thrills

I set his clock…so he can wake up and go to work early. Ha!

- Donald Kilbuck

Shaving Cream Head

It's the weekend!

Has anyone ever played *Shaving Cream Head?*

Jonnie 7-11 in foreground with James A. above.

The premise is pretty simple - just run around in public with shaving cream on your head. Aside from that, the game's details are pretty flexible. You can say inappropriate things to people or whatever. You'll find it really turns heads, even if you're just walking around minding your own business.

If you're in a small town, it's funny to urge people to try to guess who you are. Nobody will have a clue.

I'm pretty sure these photos were taken in 1991 and I'm surprised the game hasn't caught on since then.

I think it would make a good reality show.

Commentary –

Reality Show Pitch - A bunch of people from diverse backgrounds share a house in a small town and one of them is running around the community at night playing "Shaving Cream Head". Then the locals have to figure out which one of the house members it is.

- Jonnie

Jonnie, you make me very proud to know you.

- Gooseneck

The best part about this post is I HAVE played this and I got in trouble in college for it.

- Marci

(Source: I'm Nacho Steppinstone - February 27, 2004)

Fork Fangs

My cousin, Ross, taught me this in grade school at *Long John Silvers* in Fort Wayne, Indiana:

1. Start with a standard disposable plastic fork –

2. Break off the handle and center prongs, like so –

3. Flip it over –

4. Place it in your mouth, and.... ta-daaaa -

Vampire fangs!!

Note - You get maximum enjoyment from *Fork Fangs* in a public restaurant where the forks are free and there are lots of unsuspecting bystanders.

(Source: I'm Nacho Steppinstone – September 26, 2004)

Hit 'Em Again

Around the time of the 9-11 terrorist attacks, I was working the night shift at a San Bernardino gas station. The maintenance guy, Tony, used to come in at all godawful hours to get drunk in the adjoining garage since it was closed in the evenings. While Tony's late night drinking activities often led to humorous scenarios which are all worthy of recording, I think the funniest occurred right after the 9-11 terrorist attacks.

A few days after the terrorist attacks, Tony was getting drunk in the garage like usual; and a friend of his kept coming into the station and asking me, "What's Tony doing? Getting drunk?" I don't know why he gave a shit, but it seemed to really be bothering him. He came back later with a bottle of white shoe polish and said, "We should write something *fucked-up* on Tony's truck since he's in there getting *drunk*". I didn't have anything better to do, so we tossed around different ideas. U.S. patriotism was at an all time high right after 9-11, and we finally hit on the idea of a pro-Bin Laden slogan and after a few tries, we came up with the perfect thing.

As Tony pulled his truck out of the parking lot later that night, his tailgate read:

Hit 'Em Again, Bin!

It was pretty funny. Tony later said people were honking at him all the way home. He thought it was because he was driving around drunk, so he'd slow down then they'd pull up next to him and flip him the bird.

It took Tony until the next morning to figure out what "everyone's problem is".

In retrospect, I'm surprised he didn't get shot.

(Source: I'm Nacho Steppinstone - December 14, 2003)

Dashboard Dough

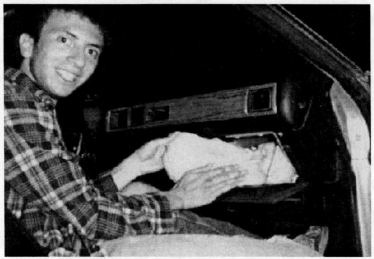

*James A. Demonstrates the Dashboard Dough Prank -
circa. 1988*

You might (but probably won't) recognize James A. from *Shaving Cream Head*. Here he is stuffing a bunch of dough into a co-worker's glove compartment.

The *Dashboard Dough* prank came about from –

(1.) having a friend who worked 3rd shift at a donut shop with lots of disposable dough, and

(2.) being broke high school kids in small town Indiana, looking for cheap thrills.

So one night we were hanging out at the donut shop making masks out of dough and the question came up, "What could we do with all this dough"?

James immediately responded, "Let's drive out to **[name witheld]**'s house and stuff it in the glove compartment of their car!"

For some reason, this seemed like a great idea at the time.

Amusing characteristics of Dashboard Dough –

1) It rises while it's sitting in the glove compartment on a hot summer night.
2) The next day, the entire car smells like beer and nobody can figure out why.
3) When the target finally opens their glove compartment, they have no idea what they're looking at or what is going on and they really freak out. They want to remove it immediately, but are afraid to touch it.

(Source: I'm Nacho Steppinstone - June 12, 2004)

Boing!

Cousin Abby bought a novelty can of nuts with the snakes that spring out when you open the lid. We plan to put it in a carry-on when we go through the airport terrorism screening line on Friday. I can't wait until the the security screeners open the can to see what's in there.

"BOING!"

hahaha.

*[**Postscript**: When we tried this, Security did not open the can. We asked the security screener why not and he said he could see the spring through the can with his x-ray. So if somebody would like to try this in the future, I would suggest a lead can.]*

(Source: I'm Nacho Steppinstone – June 02, 2004)

Your Comments:

_____

_____

_____

One Dollar

One summer when I was living in an Alaskan fish processing camp, some campsite entrepreneurs whipped up a homemade bar out of pallets and plywood scraps —

Probably the only existing photograph of the short-lived homemade campground bar, Valdez, Alaska – summer, 1991.

They bought a bunch of cheap beer, a few bottles of whiskey, and a big can of loose leaf tobacco; then announced the following offer to everybody in earshot:

One beer, One shot, One cigarette - One Dollar

Everybody was thrilled! A beer *and* a shot *and* a cigarette, for only *one dollar*! There was no proper shot glass, but huge shots were being poured into something plastic...I think it was the cap from a can of spray-on deodorant. They wouldn't roll your cigarette for you, you had to roll your own - but the price was right.

It was fun while it lasted (about 6 hours).

34

By the time the authorities shut them down, everybody on the campground had a decent buzz and the bar crew had lots of dollars. We then immediately tore the bar apart and burned it on a bonfire.

(Source: I'm Nacho Steppinstone - April 15, 2004)

Dictionary + Fire Game

One night in L.A., we entertained ourselves by building a huge bonfire in the backyard. We were all uproariously drunk and started tossing dead leaves and assorted yard debris into the fire.

As the yard started looking cleaner, our general sentiment gradually evolved into, "Let's burn all the crap we don't need" (which was A LOT of stuff). After an hour or so of tossing miscellaneous items (stained towels, ugly clothing, stuff left by overnight guests, pet kennels, old shoes, traffic cones...etc...) into the fire (now surrounded by a moat of melted plastic), somebody brought out the dictionary.

Sarah burns a nightshirt.

None of us had the heart to burn the dictionary, so we incorporated it into the game instead. We were also beginning to wonder if we'd regret burning any of this stuff the next morning, so we made up a new game on the spot.

On a rotating basis, one person would stand by the fire while the other two sat on the sidelines acting as judges. The person standing by the fire would choose an item they wanted to burn and would then make a required impromptu speech which justified the item's destruction. The final goal was to inspire applause from the judges as the item was finally tossed into the flames.

To make things more challenging though, the judges held the dictionary and whenever the speech-maker would pause for five seconds or would lose their train of thought (which was often because we were all drunk), the judges would randomly choose a word from the dictionary and yell it out at the speechmaker, who was then required to immediately incorporate the word into their speech in a coherent & meaningful context.

That was a great game and it inspired some great arguments for burning shit.

(Source: I'm Nacho Steppinstone – December 10, 2003)

Putt-Putt

One night, Sandra and I dropped by a local Miniature Golf/Water Slide/Laser Tag place. They have 5 different courses with 18 holes each and the 18th hole automatically keeps the player's ball. We bought 18 holes, then realized if we don't play the last hole, it won't keep our ball so we can play another 18 holes for free. We estimate we played 60 holes for the price of 18.

Highlights –

1) Miniature Golfing is like making love to a woman - getting it in the hole - it's best to go slowly and softly.

2) Jonnie almost lost his ball numerous times after hitting it way outside its appropriate area.

3) Sandra accidentally cut a worm in half with her putter.

4) Each hole was something special -

5) Sandra hit a kid with her golfball then, after apologizing to his mother, hit the *same* kid *again*.

6) Jonnie forgot his glasses at one of the holes, but they were returned to him by a lady (the mother of the kid who Sandra hit twice).

7) Sandra is now known as "Little Putt-Putt" to honor her considerable miniature-golf skills - she played remarkably well for somebody handicapped with a new tattoo on her ankle.

(Source: Jonnie & Sandra — September 18, 2004)

Jello Sticks

Picking up jello cubes with chopsticks is a lot harder than you might think.

Video capture of the actual event.

We guessed the jello would be fairly sticky and it would be easy, but the jello was actually impossible to grasp with chopsticks, which may be why we've never heard of anybody doing it before.

(Source: Jonnie & Sandra – September 15, 2004)

Plaster

One of the cheapest thrills of all is plaster.

You can get a big box of it at your local hardware store for probably under $2.00.

Mix it with water, soak some newspaper strips in it, let the strips dry on your face (after first applying vaseline to your face so the plaster doesn't excessively bond to your skin), and you can make custom-fitted masks.

Custom-fitted plaster masks were the brainstorm of my brother Todd way back in Indiana. He was quite a bit more ambitious than I was though, he also put plastic wrap over his hair and made a full-blown plaster helmet. He later attached newspaper horns. I just had a face-mask and my horns were held on artificially, so they sagged badly.

The Gilliom Bros. plaster mask experience.

Plaster masks are a spectacular way to kill a boring afternoon. And then later, when you're in the mood, you can sand and paint them or whatever.

Unlike many cheap thrills though, plaster lacks the instant gratification factor. There's a whole preparation process you have to attend to, then wait for the mask to dry on your face enough to remove it, then wait for the face cast to dry enough to decorate, and finally there's a huge clean-up process.

(Source: Rebel Leady Boy – April 21, 2006)

Grapette Memories

Grapette soda (readilly available at Wal-Mart) has a section on their website called *Grapette Memories* which lists selected customer memories about the soft drink.

Only happy memories though. I was disappointed the site doesn't post anecdotes automatically (they go to a screener first) because I sent in this one:

> *I recently tried Grapette for the first time and found it so delicious and affordable that I purchased two 12-packs and four 2-liter bottles. They didn't last nearly as long as I thought they would, because I couldn't stop drinking it.*
>
> *After about 4 days, I was having sharp kidney pains and (I don't know if this is related or not, but it almost HAS to be) pain in my testicles. Also, my poopy was green! And I hadn't been eating any vegetables!!*
>
> *So I took it easy awhile - the kidney pain passed pretty quickly, after I drank a lot of water. The testicle pain lasted about a week after I discontinued my Grapette consumption. And finally, after quite some time, my poopy has returned to normal.*
>
> *Perhaps I am allergic to a dye or something used in Grapette, but I really don't care. It is DELICIOUS!!*

I think we should have a contest in which we all visit Grapette's *Submit A Memory* Page and try to get one included on their website.

Commentary –

> *My fiance and I were on a month-long camping trip, just getting to know the country and getting to know each other. Before we left, we stocked up on as much Grapette as would fit in the hatchback. We made a tour of the finest car camping sites the Midwest has to offer, the Ozarks, Indiana Dunes, the Badlands.*
>
> *Along the way, we drank nothing but Grapette soda. Only thing was though -- the green-poop side effect. At first, neither of us mentioned it. But after 3*

days, and several shameless visits to campground facilities, we finally confessed to one another our secret shame. It gave us a good laugh. When we went back to drinking water, the green poop side effect went away. Now, we're married with a baby, and our week-long camping trips have nearly been forgotten -- but we'll always have this secret joke between us. Thanks for the memories, Grapette.

- Todd

haha – Did you submit that to the memory page?

- Jonnie

Yep, I sent it.

- Todd

(Source: The Real World...Blogger Style! - September 20, 2005)

Hulk Hands, 2006

Youthful Folly

I found the flow of the blue sky and white cloud, and the smoke cloud, and the sand dust, and the bite of the bumble bee when I was young.

- Donald Kilbuck

Retarded Moments

I remember once, as a boy, peeing in the backyard and suddenly getting  curious about why pee is warm and why it smelled like it did. I was in mid-stream then just aimed up and peed in my face. It wasn't an obsessive compulsion or anything like that, it was more from a sense of natural curiosity than anything else...though why I thought it was a good idea to pee in my own face, I'll never know. It made sense at the time & I'd like to clarify that I was pretty young. Like, early grade school.

Anyway, my mother happened to observe everything from our house and immediately came running out into the yard - "WHAT'S WRONG WITH YOU!!?? YOU'RE PEEING IN YOUR OWN FACE!!!!!"

I started just making shit up off the top of my head, "Well, I was peeing in the backyard and I saw a frog and bent down to look at it closer and accidentally got in the pee..."

"YOU AIMED UP AND PEED IN YOUR OWN FACE!!!"

I was grounded for the day and it must have worked because I never did it again.

I was going to share some other retarded moments, but I think that one is sufficient. I like to tell myself *everybody* has occasional retarded moments.

Commentary –

"...and I saw a frog..." - GENIUS

- Muscle68

(Source: I'm Nacho Steppinstone - January 09, 2004)

Action Men

A couple of times, when we were bored, my brother and I played *The Cosby Show* with our superhero action figures.

Malcolm Jamal Warner's character, Theo, was always played by the Hulk since the Hulk was shorter than the other action figures, just as Theo was shorter than Bill Cosby.

(Source: Boz's blog comments – http://nomoreboz.blogspot.com)

Amish Roots

Growing up in Indiana, we lived in close vicinity to an Amish community. In fact, my family shares some history with the Amish. They used to be part of the same church until there was a schism a couple hundred years ago.

I've been told that at one point in my childhood, an Amish buggy drove by the house and I took off running after it. My parents didn't know where I was, called the police & everything. Then somebody saw me chasing the buggy down the road yelling, "Horsey! Horsey!"

I told my mother I wanted to be "an Amish" when I grew up.

Commentary –

And not only that -- our Great Uncle Ralph was driving drunk with Uncle Paul and they crashed into an amish buggy.

- Todd

(Source: I'm Nacho Steppinstone – February, 2004)

Solomon W.

In Indiana, there was an Amish man named Solomon W. who would diagnose and treat ailments with herbs and folk remedies. People would come from all around the tri-state area seeking his consultation for various illnesses. He was credited with quite a few remarkable recovery stories. My Grandma Hazel used to see him regularly.

One year he sold more of one company's herbal supplements than anybody else in the country and he won a car!

But he refused it, because he was Amish.

So the herb company bought him a brand new buggy!

I used to think they ripped him off, but Grandma Hazel saw the actual buggy and claimed, "It's a real nice one".

(Source: I'm Nacho Steppinstone - February 21, 2004)

Time Capsule

When I was 14 years old, in 1984, we made a 20-year time-capsule for a class. The contents were placed in a large manilla envelope, sealed with wax, labelled "Do Not Open Until May 19, 2004", and stored with my other papers over the years until I recently realized it was past time to open it.

I vaguely remember making the time capsule and hoping I wouldn't be disappointed by the contents after waiting all those years because I didn't want to include anything that might be useful in the meantime, so the capsule just contained a lot of crap I would have thrown away otherwise.

Such as:

1.) A drawing of my cat, Meemeek:

2.) Two terrible short stories:

- The first one is titled, *The Tragic Life of Walter Locatelli* and was written on a manual typewriter. After having written everything in word processing software for the last 10 years, the hand-typed page looks pretty rugged. The story begins, "Walter Locatelli is an unhappy man. As a child, his parents tortured him in his crib"; then goes downhill fast after that. By the second paragraph, the story has already degenerated into gibberish. If I remember correctly, the part about being tortured in the crib was a classmate's suggestion; so I really had nothing to do with the most remarkable part of that story, the remaining gibberish was all mine though.

- The second story isn't as good as the first. It's a war story - "They killed some of our guys, but we killed more of theirs. My partner, Alvin, was shot down. He owed me $12.00, but his wallet was in his pocket floating over the horizon with the rest of his bottom half; so I started swimming that way too, looking for it".

(Source: I'm Nacho Steppinstone - Tuesday, December 07, 2004)

1984 Revisited

My time capsule also contained a journal which includes an eclectic selection of commentary relevant to all spheres of life –

Popular Slogans of the Day - *Get laid in an arcade!*

Personal Recollections - *...the glory of killing a chicken...*

Fiction - *Tapioca was spinning through space, imprisoned on a love asteroid.*

Economic Speculation - *My collection of Encyclopedia Brown books will be worth a fortune.*

Social Observation - *Jock Itch is the fad of the '80s.*

Cultural Criticism - *There are a lot of druggies in North America, not to mention John Cougar.*

(Source: Rebel Leady Boy - January 29, 2006)

Your Comments:

_____

_____

_____

_____

_____

_____

_____

Selected Journal Entries
(from March-April, 1984)

Today was a good day because nobody told me what to do and we all got along fine.

I don't like how I look.
I prayed about it, but nothing happened.
I don't know what else to do.

Tomorrow is class. I hope I look good, because I haven't looked good in class even one time all year.

We went to a fish fry. It was fun, even though nobody from my class was there.

In gym class, James was making fun of me for not having much hair on my legs. I, myself, don't feel that having hairy legs is important at all...maybe I shouldn't even be his friend anymore.

I didn't go to church today and I'm glad.
It's not that I don't believe in God, it's just that churches give me a real bad feeling.

I had a good day today. We didn't do anything in gym class...if tomorrow goes like I plan, tomorrow will be just as good.

Grandma Roth gave me a new shirt - it has the name of her church on it.

Nick and I stole 2 of Uncle Rick's rubbers when we were over there for Easter. We put one in a guy's mailbox and saved the other until today when we sold it to a kid at church for a dollar.

I got a new pair of jeans at the mall. All is well and I have no problems.

Today I worked in the school cafeteria and almost got fired for throwing a milk in the air & letting it land in the meat balls.

I guess there's nothing else to say, except good-bye.

Commentary –

I can't believe I was so vain. Later in life, I learned hairy legs are, in fact, pretty important though.

- Jonnie

It's not vanity when you're 14.

- Todd

(Source: I'm Nacho Steppinstone - Thursday, December 09, 2004)

Seven Stupid Dreams

What does a 14 year old dream about?
My time capsule might have some clues, it contains a short dream notebook from March, 1984.

Some sample entries –

- *I was watching a cable TV station that was all about video games.*
- *I was at Nick's house and he had a cup full of liquid vitamin C. We were dipping chips in it.*
- *I went to a martial arts class, but when I walked into the building, everybody was just sitting on benches looking around. Then the teacher came in and made us read from a computer book. It didn't have anything to do with martial arts at all.*
- *We were getting ready for church & a lady from the church was telling us about their Sunday School. I kept imagining her naked while she was talking and I wanted to have sex with her.*
- *Aunt Denise gave me and Todd a bunch of old comic books, a bunch of new records, and a Hall & Oats tape.*
- *Deb gave Mark 2 plastic bags full of pink stuff.*
- *I was running down some stairs really fast, looking for the bathroom, but couldn't find it anywhere. Then I went outside and there was a man with a black beard. He gave me a skull.*

(Source: I'm Nacho Steppinstone - December 08, 2004)

Momentum

When I was a little kid, I remember one night when we were trying to emulate Evel Knievel's greatness at my cousins' house. We lined up a bunch of toy cars and trucks next to a ping pong table (Tonka trucks, Matchbox cars, the G.I. Joe helicopter, whatever we could find) and I planned to drive my cousin's Big Wheel off the ping pong table, jumping over the entire line of cars and trucks in the process.

We spent a lot of time debating how many cars I could probably jump and whether the line of cars was too long or could be extended. I was pretty confident I could fly a fairly long distance since I could ride the Big Wheel really fast out on the sidewalk.

We put no thought into the need for ramps or for building up speed, or for anything really; besides how many cars I could probably jump.

So we placed the cars in a long line and hoisted the Big Wheel up on top of the ping pong table. I climbed up on the table, then onto the Big Wheel, turned the peddles maybe two rotations, and BAM! - fell straight down on my face! I don't think the Big Wheel's back wheels ever even left the table.

So that's how I learned about the importance of momentum.

(Source: I'm Nacho Steppinstone – June 19, 2004)

Your Comments:

Pinewood Derby

I did a brief stint in the *Cub Scouts of America* (circa 2nd or 3rd grade, late 1970s). Pretty much the only thing I remember is the pinewood derby - you could buy standardized pinewood blocks with wheel kits, then fashion them into a car with sanding tools. Then all the Cub Scouts would race them at a big annual event.

My pinewood derby car, painted in cubscout blue & gold.

My father was a lot more excited about the race than I was. This was when he was still drinking and I remember he melted down a bunch of lead fishing sinkers, drilled two long holes into the front of the car, then filled the holes with the molten lead.

The idea was to make the car heavier than the other cars so it would win (the racetrack ran downhill).

Then he sealed the lead filled holes with wood putty and painted the circles yellow like headlights; but that drew too much attention to the holes so he just painted the whole front with a thick coat of yellow instead.

It turned out I had the date of the race confused though, so I missed it and I'm glad because another Cub Scout told me they weighed the cars beforehand, so I would've been busted if I had attended, which would've been embarrassing.

(Source: I'm Nacho Steppinstone - April 10, 2005)

Young Jonnie as Batman.

Autobiographical Accounts

Cash is good! With all my emotional cash shortage my wallet is empty. I feel fine even though i am broke i still have my truck to drive around with.

- Donald Kilbuck

P-E-P-S-I S-P-I-R-I-T

The earliest bottlecap contest I remember was Pepsi's *Pepsi Spirit* game in which each bottle cap had a letter printed on the inside and the goal was for consumers to collect the appropriate letters to spell *Pepsi Spirit*. It was back before plastic twist-off caps were common and opening a Pepsi required you to pop the metal cap with a bottle opener.

The *R* was the one universally rare piece, though I didn't know it at the time. I was just a kid and I figured there must be equal numbers of each piece and for all I knew, the *E* was the hard one to get and we already had several of those.

I'd excitedly tell people, "We have all of them but the *R*"! and they'd roll their eyes at me.

At one gas station, the attendent used a marker to make a *P* into an *R* and had the caps sitting out by his cash register, as if he were missing a different letter.

We were like, "WHOA! You have the *R*!! We have the *E*! We should go in together and split the money!"

Then he laughed and pointed out it was a fake *R* and was actually about the 5th one he made because people kept grabbing his fake *R* and running out the door with it!

I always thought making the fake *R* and sitting it out in public was a pretty funny prank.

(Source: Rebel Leady Boy – May 18, 2006)

Your Comments:

_____

_____

_____

57

Chili Dog Burrito

As ridiculous as it may sound, this is totally true -

Back in the mid-'80s, before the *Taco Bell* resurgence, burritos were not all that popular in the Midwest. The first burritos I ever ate were frozen ones from the supermarket, before burritos were even widely available in convenience stores.

Our supermarket's frozen brand was available in three varieties - *Red Hot* in a red wrapper, *Mild* in a green wrapper, and *Chili Dog* in a brown wrapper.

I loved *Red Hot* and *Mild*, but *Chili Dog* was introduced later and I was unfamiliar with it the first (and only) time I tried one. I guessed it would be full of beefy chili dog style chili or something.

I'll never forget my shock the first time I bit into it – The burrito had a whole hot dog in there! It was a hotdog encased in beans, then wrapped in a tortilla and frozen! It was SO unnatural! I was probably 12 or 13 years old and I think I shrieked out loud when I bit in and pulled out a hot dog.

I don't know whose idea that was, but I'm really glad it never caught on.

Commentary –

That is just wrong on so many levels.

- Kat

(Source: I'm Nacho Steppinstone – June 20, 2004)

Burrito Freakout

I generally maintain a pretty even temper, but a recent discussion regarding sudden outbursts of irrational/emotional behavior got me thinking about my own experiences in that area.

There aren't too many of them; I'm not quick to fly off the handle over anything. I've handled a lot of crazy situations with absolute cool-headedness.

That being said, those of you who know me probably won't be too surprised to learn that I once seriously lost it because my burrito fell apart.

It was the late '80s, I was in high school and had just lovingly made myself a burrito at home using the last of some leftovers from the refrigerator.

I made myself comfortable, had my napkin and everything I could possibly need; sat down in an easy chair - added salsa, picked the burrito up, brought it to my mouth - and the tortilla split apart!!

Spilled the contents all over the plate.

It pissed me off so much that I punched the living room window - *and shattered it.* Which was stupid because then there was glass in my burrito too.

I don't think anything's ever pissed me off so much in my life.

I would be ashamed of myself if not for the affection I hold for human stupidity.

Commentary –

"[...] a recent discussion regarding sudden outbursts of irrational/ emotional behavior [...]".

Irrational?! Since I think I know what you're referring to... DON'T YOU EVER DARE TO LAUGH AGAIN WHEN I TELL YOU THAT I

CRIED OVER SPILLED COFFEE!!!!! It was a fuckin caramel latte macchiato with extra cream and not some ordinary coffee and I spilled almost half of the cup. And the other half was DELICIOUS which made my pain so much worse!

- Sandra

Oh, I didn't know it was caramel. I stand corrected. It was entirely rational in that case.

- Jonnie

I once dropped a frozen Snickers bar in the sand, I didn't get mad, I just picked it up, wiped it off the best I could and ate it. It was kind of crunchy. Jonnie, I think there is a lesson for you to be learned here.

- Boz

Yes, Jonnie, and that lesson is that Boz eats sand.

- Kat

Boz is trying to trick me into eating glass, again.

- Jonnie

Yesterday I threw a glass plate at the wall because I needed to smash something (the unoffending trigger- a quesadilla) but it was made of safety glass or some shit, and it didn't break. What's even worse than getting emotional? CATHARSIS INTERRUPTUS. I'm STILL PISSED!

- AmyJo

That's horrible! There's nothing more satisfying than shattering dishes against the wall. I don't know what I'd do if I threw a shatterproof one. I honestly don't...

- Jonnie

(Source: I'm Nacho Steppinstone - May 07, 2004)

A Whole Different Sandwich

In the early 1990s, I briefly worked at Burger King to pay the bills while I looked for a better job. During this time, BK was offering their Whopper for 99 cents where it was normally $2.25 or something like that. The Whopper with Cheese, however, retained it's original price of $2.49 because the manager claimed it was a "whole different sandwich" and was not subject to the regular Whopper discount.

And that put me (a counter person) in some awkward situations.

It was a customer service nightmare because people kept ordering the 99 cent Whopper and requesting cheese on it, then freaking out when they were charged $2.49 instead of the expected $1.09. They'd look at me in disbelief and say, "You're charging me $1.50 for a piece of cheese"?

Then the worst part was when I had to say, "Yes we are" and explained to them that the Whopper with Cheese was a whole different sandwich which was not on sale at this time.

haha - I never felt like such a douchebag in my life.
And in that stupid hat too.

(Source: Rebel Leady Boy - May 14, 2006)

Broke Down

Here's one of many past roadside breakdown photos –

This was in the parking lot of a NAPA auto parts store in Bozeman, Montana during a 1994 roadtrip from Indiana to Alaska. We were catching our leaking antifreeze in pans because we feared NAPA would kick us off their property if we flooded their lot with antifreeze.

As bad as that may have seemed, events quickly got worse. Among other things, our camp stove stopped working. While my brother, Todd, was dealing with the leaking radiator, I was troubleshooting the camp stove with our travel companion, Laura. Somehow, I caught the can of kerosene I was holding on fire. It's pretty explosive stuff. And then events escalated fast.

I looked down and saw flames around the can's nozzle and unthinkingly hurled the can at the NAPA building where it exploded almost immediately. I didn't intend to throw it directly *at* the NAPA building. I just instinctually threw it *away* from our van.

At any rate, here's the result –

The explosion riled the store staff more than antifreeze in their parking lot *ever* could. They came running outside with fire extinguishers!

Brother Todd saw the explosion and immediately threw the van in neutral to get away from the fire. He coasted downhill, right over all those pans of antifreeze. Laura peed her pants from laughing so hard. I took pictures for posterity.

(Source: I'm Nacho Steppinstone – February 10, 2004)

Hyderization

During that same Alaskan roadtrip, we'd been driving up through British Columbia, Canada for what seemed like forever.

The proper entrance to Alaska is through the Yukon Territory, which was still hundreds of miles North. We heard about a southern Alaskan town called Hyder, accessible from British Columbia. There are no roads to Alaska's interior from Hyder, it's just an isolated town in the middle of nowhere. You have to backtrack on the road you drove in on then continue up through Canada to reach Alaska's road system.

We were road weary from days of driving and decided it was worth the 200 mile detour to check it out since it was a unique opportunity. I mean, who goes to Hyder? It's absolutely in the middle of nowhere. At any rate, it had to be better than sitting in the van another day.

Hyder was pretty much what we expected - a tiny little town - a few buildings (two-thirds of which were bars) and a lot of mud.

Welcome to Hyder.

What's interesting about Hyder is the total absence of customs officials when crossing the U.S.-Canada border.

We went right through without any incident. I guess because once you're in Hyder, there's no way of getting any further, so a border patrol would be considered a waste of time.

According to one local, Hyder did try to establish a border patrol office at some point in the town's history, but the locals "shot it up".

There was nothing there anymore, we weren't even sure where Canada ended & Alaska began. There were no signs or anything.

Again, a local - "There used to be a sign, but it fell down, eh?"

The *Glacier Inn* bar provided a welcome break from the road. The walls were covered with autographed money, originally from miners staking their claims, but in recent years it was probably just drunks.

I don't recall if any of us put money on the wall. I'd think we probably did, but then I think I would've taken a picture of it if we had. I do remember playing pool though.

The *Glacier Inn* promoted a tradition called "Hyderization", which consisted of drinking a shot of everclear then receiving a commemorative card signed and dated by the bartender.

Here's mine —

THIS IS TO CERTIFY
THAT I _Jas. R. Keller_
HAVE BEEN HYDERIZED
BY THE GLACIER INN
HYDER ALASKA
DATE 5/23/94 SIGNED _Keller_

Just wanted to scrapbook Hyder - drop by if you're ever in the middle of nowhere. It was pretty fun.

Commentary –

i think i live there.

- Zann

(I'm Nacho Steppinstone – March 12, 2004)

First Impressions

When I recently arrived in Anchorage and was getting on my feet, I bought a van real cheap from a co-worker who I later learned was also a crack dealer. It was a pretty fun van to drive - there was a huge Malcolm X banner hanging in the back and a bunch of wooden beads colored like the African flag hanging from the rearview mirror; not something a white guy generally drives around town. It really turned heads on occasion.

So eventually, I took a job working with disabled kids. On my first day, I drove that van and I remember having a completely overbearing head cold at the time. I was in the back of the van looking for some kleenex and found this huge caliber sawed-off shotgun in the back! I don't know what I was thinking (I was ill and disoriented at the time), but I picked it up, pulled the trigger (I guess to see if it worked) and BLAMMM!!

65

Blew a hole right through the side of my new van. Right in the parking lot of the house I was going to work in on my first day! I just remember my ears ringing like crazy and the smell of gunpowder. I'm glad nobody was outside in the parking lot! The lady who ran the house came running out and asked me what was going on. All I could think about was my headcold and I didn't want to explain it all to her, so I stupidly stuck my head out the window, held up the shotgun and said, "I just shot a hole in my van. I have a headcold", as if that explained anything at all.

She didn't say a word, went back in the house. I came in a little later and started my first shift. We later became fairly good aquaintences, but she NEVER mentioned the incident as long as I knew her. Pretty easy going lady.

The above illustration is brother Todd holding his Swiss Army knife by the shotgun hole for scale. The shot wasn't too far from hitting the gas tank. That would've been a mess.

(Source: Rebel Leady Boy - February 13, 2006)

4th Avenue

I don't spend much time in bars these days, but I used to hang out there all the time. I wish I had half the money I've pissed away in bars.

My favorite spot was Anchorage's 4th Avenue district, they had a great selection of cheap working class bars there, nevermind the occasional shooting. In my mind at the time, 4th Avenue was a magical place where anything could happen. I used to have a ton of 4th Avenue bar stories, but I've forgotten most of them. They never held up too well once sobriety set in. The music wasn't too loud (when there was music at all), so you could better listen to people talking shit.

I'd always tell people how great the 4th Avenue bars were, then they'd join me and nothing interesting would happen. That's about when I realized my ton of 4th Avenue bar stories was more the result of my hanging out there constantly, rather than anything to do with the bars themselves. If you hang out *anywhere* day and night, you're bound to witness a few strange occurances.

(I'm Nacho Steppinstone - December 22, 2004)

California, Here We Come

When I left Alaska at the end of 1999, I wanted to go somewhere fun, so I chose Las Vegas. I've been thinking today about when we left Las Vegas in the middle of the night a few years ago and came to California.

My apartment manager in Vegas was one of these guys who tried to control every aspect of his wife's life. He'd keep her paycheck, she had to ask permission to use the phone, all sorts of nonsense. My apartment was right next to theirs and I'd frequently hear all kinds of altercations

I hadn't accomplished anything productive during my five months in Vegas and agreed to help my friend, Gina, relocate to California where her mother owned a house. In exchange for transportation assistance, Gina would provide me with a guest shed where I could live cheaply in her back yard. Up until that point, Vegas had just been lots of hanging around in casinos and bars for me, so I saw the chance to "justify" my time there by performing a good deed in offering the apartment manager's wife an opportunity to escape her ugly situation. Surprisingly, she actually took me up on it.

The apartment manager started getting crazier and crazier, walking around with guns and peeking in windows. So it was clear we needed to leave immediately before he got violent. One day, the girl kept him out on the town while Gina & I moved our furnishings and personal possessions to a third party's apartment for storage. We then returned to the apartment complex as if everything were normal. Nobody had any idea our apartments were completely empty inside.

One night, the girl went over to "visit Gina" and they snuck out the back door to my car across the street in the Tropicana hotel's parking lot. I walked out my front door a little later (right by the apartment manager who was staring out his window at me the whole time) and met them there. I was carrying a gym bag with the last of my personal items in it – toothbrush, toothpaste, some dirty laundry, and my telephone. Then we dropped by the third party's apartment, loaded our stuff in a U-Haul, and drove straight to California.

All I left behind in my apartment was the furniture that came with the place. The apartment manager lent me a few things over the months - some headphones, a couple of CDs. I was sure to leave these behind as well since I didn't want him to have any legal recourse in following me (rent, for example, was completely up to date).

The clincher occurred to me while cleaning out my kitchen pantry. I had a huge bag of bulk dried black beans and you know how when the bag tears, they fall all over the place? I sliced the bottom open and left the bag perched on the edge of the upper pantry shelf. So when the apartment manager was going through the apartment later and lifted the bag to throw it away - a shower of beans!!!!

(Source: I'm Nacho Steppinstone – December 23, 2003)

Learning Stick

I stumbled across this email I sent to brother Todd (dated May 31, 2000) which contains a detailed description of my first experience driving a manual transmission. I remember I was working in a factory at that time and the foreman offered me a forklift driver job if I went through forklift training over the weekend. My full account reads something like this -

I went to forklift training this weekend and all they had was a stick shift, which I had no idea how to drive. It was pretty bad and the instructor was pretty cranky. I about ran the forklift through his wall and I kept laughing whenever I screwed something up, which was making the guy get madder and madder. In all my preoccupation over how to use the clutch without killing the machine, I kept forgetting the basic forklift safety video he'd just showed us. Looking behind you before going in reverse is very important, of course, because you could run into somebody; but it was far from my mind while I was learning how to drive a stick for the first time (in front of an audience no less). Whenever I'd back up without looking, he'd yell, "You just killed somebody!!" and then I'd laugh really hard because he was so high strung. I was trying to concentrate on not letting the machine die and safety stuff was secondary to me. I also didn't tell him I didn't know how to drive a stick in the first place, so he thought I was just really a fuck-up.

He kept saying, "OK, I should tear up your license right now, but if you can move that crate and put it up on that shelf without fucking anything up, I'll let you have your license".

I'd say, "Alright" then take a deep breath thinking about how to work the forks and keep from killing the machine. I'd get oriented and start backing up, then he'd go "YOU JUST KILLED SIX PEOPLE!!!"

Then I'd laugh really hard and say, "I didn't mean to!"

I finally told him I'd never driven a stick before and he said, "oh, well, you should learn."

69

One other guy left before his test because he'd never driven a stick before either. After watching me and the instructor for awhile, he just snuck out the door and disappeared.

Anyway, there's a happy ending. The instructor told me I'd not get my license and to come back next week for more training (I was thinking, "Damn. So much for getting that forklift job then"). Then he took me into his office where he was really cool (I guess he was just acting like a hardass in front of the group). His associate said this sort of thing happens all the time and not to worry about it. The instructor told his associate to put my license on the bulletin board until next week when I would return to earn it, then he went out for the next class.

When he left, the associate said, "Don't worry about it", signed the license and then looked at the bulletin board and said, "There's so much stuff up there. I don't think we'd be able to find your license. It might get lost...I wonder where I could put it so it wouldn't get lost...{wink wink}...Here, I'll give it to you to hold on to and then you bring it back with you next week...{wink wink}...

I thanked him then left immediately...What a cool guy!

When I returned to the factory on Monday, I was SO NERVOUS about driving the forklift on the job. Then I found out it was a automatic, so I'm fine...whew!

This experience came in handy about a year and a half later. I was working in a gas station and taking a bus to work because my car had broken down. The gas station's owner used to buy old vehicles to fix-up and re-sell. One day he showed up to drive me to work in an old pick-up truck he was trying to re-sell. On the way to work, he said I could keep the pick-up for getting to and from work until he sold it. He was just a cool guy like that. He didn't pay much in wages, but he took pretty good care of you if you were halfway competent.

Almost immediately after I thanked him, I realized the truck was a stick shift and I'd never driven a stick in my life (aside from my forklift training fiasco). But I was afraid if I mentioned anything about that, he wouldn't let me borrow the truck, so I kept my mouth shut.

As we pulled into the station, I (very cleverly, in my opinion) requested he park in the back (away from public view) so I could check the fluids and whatnot. And right there behind the station is where I taught myself to drive stick. Once I could get it to accelerate without killing it, I pulled it off the lot and took it down a sidestreet (away from anybody who might know me) and gave myself a crash course.

(Source: Rebel Leady Boy – March 14, 2006)

Hit By a Train

Shooting my van wasn't the stupidest thing I've done either. The stupidest was getting hit by a train in San Bernardino.

There's not much I could say to explain it. It was just stupid.

I was wandering around by the tracks (in no condition to be out in public) thinking about how bad San Bernardino sucked, when I decided, "The next train going East...I'm gonna jump on that fucker and get out of here". I had serious bridge burning tendencies in those days.

I was standing by a normal stretch of track, nowhere near a station & trains go FAST once they get rolling, but I'd psyched myself up too much and I just *had* to try it.

A train came by eventually and I was by the track and I remember thinking, "It's going REALLY fast...I don't know...."

Next thing I remember, I'm in a hospital bed with a bunch of nurses around me. I can only guess what happened. I don't know if I actually attempted the jump or if I just staggered too close and got whacked by a ladder or something hanging on the side; but somebody saw me by the track and called an ambulance. They said I was completely covered in blood.

When I regained consciousness, I was in a hospital I never heard of with a broken arm and staples in my head and leg. It was a day or so later and nobody knew where I was or what happened. A friend of mine called all the police stations & hospitals until she finally located me. I was heavily sedated and I only remember telling her, "Pick me up. Get me out of here". I remember thinking it was Monday, and being totally surprised to learn it was actually Wednesday.

I didn't have any medical insurance however, so I really just got minimal care. After my release, they wanted me to go back at least twice per week for follow-up exams at $50 - $100/visit. I politely accepted then never called them again. When everything started healing, I removed the cast from my arm and pulled the staples out of my head and leg with a pair of needlenose pliers. And that is when I knew I was freaking hardcore for sure.

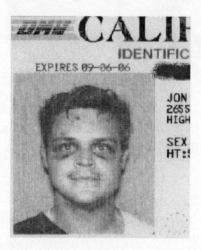

New DMV I.D., post train incident.

So after that I stopped getting so drunk in public, toned down the drinking in general. Being hit by a train and surviving uses up a lot of one's luck. It's a miracle things didn't end tragically that night.

Lesson Learned - *The train is not a toy.*

Commentary –

I'd hate to see the damage to the train.

- Maxine

I'm sure the train was in a bad, bad way

- Jonnie

(Source: I'm Nacho Steppinstone – December 18, 2003)

Office Party

I had no intention of attending the company Christmas party, but my boss is shrewd. First, she mentioned Christmas bonuses and prize drawings (still not interested). NOW they're giving out paychecks *at* the Christmas party. If you skip the Xmas party, the office is closed the rest of the week and you have no paycheck....OK, so I *am* going to the company Christmas party. Ready to walk out the door right now. I'm bringing my present for the gift exchange. It's a hand flipping the bird. Can't wait to see who the lucky recipient is.

Front View   *Back View*

Commentary –

That's an actual gift? Are you asking to be fired?

- Paul

I'm planning to get a new job anyway after I move to the OC next month. As things turned out though, I'm keeping the finger for myself.

- Jonnie

(Source: I'm Nacho Steppinstone – December 22, 2003)

Jonnie Homemaker

I'm out of LA and all settled in the OC. I just spent $100 on bathroom, cleaning, & office supplies.

The cleaning products will probably last me for years.

I also replenished some essentials - new towels, wine corkscrew, a bathroom rug that's pleasing to the bare feet, toilet plunger w/ an ergonomic handle (!), and some of that shit that makes your toilet water blue.

I think I'm ready to roll.

Commentary –

What is it about pissing in a blue water toilet that is so soothing? Especially in your own home...

- Gooseneck

(I'm Nacho Steppinstone - January 28, 2004)

Central Air

I've never been a huge fan of the sun, and since I've moved to the west coast, I've really hated the long hot summers.

At first I thought it was because I came down from Alaska and hadn't properly adjusted to the climate. But now, four years later, I still hate them.

My first year and half in California was spent living in my friend Gina's shed, which was actually very comfortable (for a shed). I had a huge rug for carpet, cable TV, and a microwave, but summers were a bitch. No ventilation at all. And mice. You couldn't beat the price though, it was just freaking hot in the summer.

My current system involves an air conditioning vent outlet right in my room. It blasts cool air directly into a rotating ceiling fan which stirs it all up.

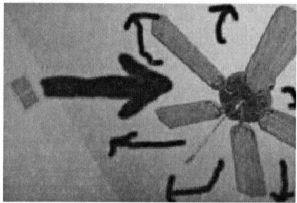

Much like a blender.

I predict this will be the first California summer where I truly have nothing to bitch about. So if you catch me bitching, remind me I have air conditioning & a pool.

(Source: I'm Nacho Steppinstone - May 03, 2004)

Labor Ready Revisited

I only register with Labor Ready when I absolutely have to, like when I arrive in a new town and need a little dough while I'm getting on my feet. If you don't mind hard physical work, it's a reliable means of getting some quick cash (though not much) while you're waiting for something better to come along.

Yesterday I decided, instead of hanging around the house all day, I should behave like the man of action I am. I've been getting stagnant lately in front of the computer all the time for school, work, *and* recreation. I felt the need to revisit old reliable *Labor Ready*.

I went down and applied yesterday. This morning, I was assigned to an earthmoving company. In practice, we were actually picking up huge rocks all day, which really sucked. But then again, I *have* been complaining about my need for exercise - so I got a lot of that at least.

I've always felt it was important to experience as many diverse types of people as possible and it did me good to get around the Labor Ready crowd again. It kind of put things in perspective after interacting solely with library types lately.

Early morning at my local L.R. branch – located next to the 'World of Warriors' Vintage Gun shop.

Today's Labor Ready Report –

I transported 3 other laborers to the job site and got an extra $2 from each for gas. Co-worker #1 was kind of nuts, kept talking about how he's gonna make a pipe bomb for 4th of July.

Co-worker #2 was a good enough guy, though he'd had hard luck lately. His wife is taking a good chunk of his lousy wages for child support. He just got out of prison, where he was serving time for beating a guy up with an aluminum baseball bat because, "I told him to get out of my house, but he didn't go".

But the day did suck, because they gave no breaks (not even lunch) and it was heavy duty work right there in the sun, I thought I was gonna pass out, but didn't. But we got in 9 hours, and I was paid less than what I get for screwing around a few hours on webpages from the comfort of my own home, and my body was beat…but it was good to go back and see what I'm missing again.

Rebel Leady Boy

We apparently did an acceptable job, they invited us back tomorrow, though neither of my co-workers are going. And I don't blame them, it really was back breaking work, for lousy pay.

I think I will do at least one more day....it did me good to get out in a different environment, even if it sucked. Got a ton of exercise and a little walking around money without the daily time commitment of a straight job.

(Source: I'm Nacho Steppinstone – June 30, 2004)

Coyotes In These Here Hills

Despite urbanization efforts, coyotes still roam around here at night. One of them grabbed a dog right in its own yard.

I'll try to get a picture of one by the lemon tree.

(Source: I'm Nacho Steppinstone – February 16, 2004)

Pantsless in the OC

Absent Mindedness has never been a huge problem for me, though it does occur from time to time. Usually it manifests as forgetting what I was saying in mid-sentence or walking into things.

Today though, I reached unprecedented heights of absent mindedness. I was way nervous during a job interview today (via telephone). Before the interview, I was sure to get fully dressed, so I wouldn't come off as too casual from lounging around in my pajamas.

I remember at one point thinking my belt felt too tight.

Then I just totally got into the interview and I think it went reasonably well. But after I hung up the phone, I realized I had taken my pants off (!!) Without ever realizing it!!

They were sitting there on the floor and I conducted the last part of my interview in my socks and underwear. I don't remember removing my pants at all!

Nothing like this has ever happened before and I hope it doesn't become a trend. Thank god it wasn't a face-to-face interview.

I really hope it was only a one-time thing.

(Source: Rebel Leady Boy – February 21, 2006)

Interpersonal

I seen Dale walking somewheres and i told him he owes me three hundred [dollars] and he seemed to think that he really does owe me three hundred...Spaced Out!

- Donald Kilbuck

Sandra in L.A. :

"Oh My God! Look At All the Trucks!"

My Liebling, Sandra, arrived from Germany on Tuesday morning at 12:12 a.m. and I must say I'm not disappointed at all. Our personalities are almost identical so there is no awkwardness whatsoever, though there was a little initial nervousness. So far, it couldn't be more perfect.

Jonnie & Sandra at Laguna Beach.

Yesterday was spent adjusting to the time and climate change. We browsed around Orange and stocked up on snacks and necessities at the 99 cent store (*six bags* of stuff for $23.00! Including a terrible rap cassette we both agreed we would have paid $20.00 for, so it's like everything else only cost $3.00).

Then we returned home and screwed around in the pool where Sandra discovered I can't float and I, "swim like a puppy". So there's the first dent in my hardcore persona.

I predicted in this age of international culture, it would be mundane details that most impressed a visitor to America, things so prevalent that we don't even notice them here. I think I was right, because, on the drive home from the airport, one of the first things out of Sandra's mouth was, "Oh my God!!! Look at all the trucks!!!!"

I learned that England is world famous for its potato chips (or "crisps"), Sandra bought a bunch of them at the London airport - all kinds of exotic flavors (or "indulgent flavors" as one label stated) - "roasted chicken with thyme", "grilled steak with peppercorn", and I don't know what all. I'm glad she likes chips as much as I do. In fact, when she entered the U.S., the only thing she had to declare to customs was two bags of English crisps.

(Source: I'm Nacho Steppinstone – July 21, 2004)

Your Comments:

---

99 Cent Anecdote

When I first introduced Sandralein to Brandee, the owner of the house I rent from; it went something like this:

Brandee: "Nice to meet you! Did he take you out and show you the area"?

Sandra: "Yes"!

Brandee: "Did he take you to Disney World"?

Sandra: "No, but he took me to the 99 Cent Store".

Then Brandee just looked at me like I was a real cheap-ass.

She didn't understand though that neither of us were the slightest bit interested in visiting Disney World. We are much more interested in value.

(Source: The 99 Cent Blog - February 25, 2006)

Sandra with Alaskan Moose Nightlight from Papa Jon.

Travelling Exhibit

Sandralein whipped up this drawing (in only about an hour's time!) for *The Real World...Blogger Style's* first anniversary and I thought it was so great I would print it here.

From left to right: Rosa Posa, Dvl, Mad Mathias, Marci, Sandra, Jonnie, Boz, Belle, AmyJo, Drew, Nancy, CJ, Cori.

It features the *Real World...Blogger Style!* members as participants in the Biblical "Last Supper", the role of Christ is played by Boz, of course:

Here's my favorite detail –

Jonnie Kissing the Artist (Sandra) [with Marci in foreground].

Good Job, Liebling - It's a masterpiece!!

(Source: I'm Nacho Steppinstone – April 02, 2005)

Jay, the Former Carnie

This summer, I'm working with a guy named Jay. In addition to being a former carnie, Jay is also a barrel of laughs. I took notes yesterday and recorded four specific incidents in which Jay made me laugh:

1.) RE: Walking into the breakroom and finding Ambush Makeovers on the television -

Jay: "Fuck this! I don't wanna see an ambush makeover!"

[changes station to Judge Joe Brown]

Jay: "I wanna see someone get hung!!"

Jonnie: "hahahaha"

2.) RE: "Day-O" by Harry Belefonte -

Jay: "Come Mr. Tallyman, Tally me banana" - You know what that means, don't you?"

Jonnie: "He wants the foreman to count his bananas so he can get paid and go home."

Jay: "NOoo - well, ok, maybe...but what it *really* means is he wants a guy to measure his dick."

Jonnie: "HAHAHA"

Jay: "Well, yeah, 'tally my banana'! That's what it *means.*"

Jonnie: "hahahaha"

3.) RE: Spider Venom Contest –

Jay: "Did you know the Daddy Long Legs is the most venomous spider in the world?"

Jonnie: "No."

86

Jay: "Yep, but its fangs are so small, they can't break your skin."

Jonnie: "huh!"

Jay: "Look it up! Or watch the Discovery Channel!!"

Jonnie: "ok."

Jay: "And I've *always* wanted to put a Daddy Long Legs and a Black Widow in a jar together and see which one would walk out alive."

Jonnie: "YEAH! I want to see too!! Let's do it here at work!"

Jay: "OK, keep your eyes peeled for a Black Widow and a Daddy Long Legs. And a jar. And keep your gloves on".

Jonnie: "HAHAHAHAHA...OK!"

4. RE: Family Illness -

Jay: "Yeah, his [Jay's brother's] liver's got some damage and he might have to check into the hospital. I really hope not though. I hope he feels better soon and *doesn't* have to go to the hospital because I really don't like to pray. I prayed once already today."

Jonnie: "I hear *that.*"

Commentary –

Today's big lunch discussion was, "What would you do if you looked down *right now* and there was a rattlesnake?"

Jay said he's always wanted to catch a rattlesnake and if he did, he'd skin it and make a headband out of the skin (with the rattle hanging off the back).

- Jonnie

I give Jay a ride back to the Rebel Leady office after work and yesterday's Jay monologue went something like this:

Jay: "Did you know the fly is the only animal that can be frozen and then brought back to life?"

Jonnie: "Really?"

Jay: "Yep - on the Discovery channel they froze one, then thawed it out later and it came back to life".

Jonnie: "Like Captain Ameria!"

Jay: "Exactly! Freeze me solid and thaw me out in the year 3000! Or better yet, freeze me and thaw me out once there's a cure for AIDS!!"

Jonnie: "hahahaha"

- Jonnie

Jay: "The only other animal that can be frozen and brought back to life is the lobster. You can freeze a lobster solid, then throw it in boiling water and the fucker will scream every time! You killed him once, now you're killing him again!!...Imagine doing that to a human!"

- Jonnie

I was giving Jay a ride home and we were behind a car with a license plate that said "BIBL NRD".

Jonnie: "Bible Nerd!"

Jay: [looks really puzzled] "Well, I can understand, "Bible FANATIC" or something like that, but "Bible Nerd" is kind of OUT THERE!"

Jonnie: "Let's follow him."

Jay: "If you follow *him*, I'm getting out and walking."

- Jonnie

(Source: *Rebel Leady Boy* – July 16, 2005)

Knecht Ruprecht

Sandra and I were comparing German and American Christmas traditions this morning and Santa has an *enforcer* in Germany named Knecht Ruprecht.

Sandra: we don't have Santa Claus

Sandra: we have the "Christkind"

Jonnie: Really?

Sandra: we call Santa Claus "Nikolaus" and he comes on december 6

Jonnie: what does he bring?

Sandra: depends on whether you've been good over the year

Sandra: if you were good, you'll (traditionally) get fruits, Lebkuchen, almonds and nuts and stuff like that... today he brings chocolate and a little present

Sandra: if you were bad, you'll get hit

Jonnie: He hits you???

Sandra: no, he got a helper who does that

Jonnie: that's funny!

Sandra: Knecht Ruprecht

Jonnie: hahaha

Jonnie: Does he look mean?

Sandra: YES

Sandra: he got a birch

Jonnie: hahaha

Sandra: wait, I'll try to find a pic

Jonnie: oh my god, he looks like that picture of the Unabomber!

Sandra: unabomber?

Jonnie: He blew up a federal building or something - he looked exactly like Knecht Ruprecht

Sandra: Aaaaaaaaaaahhhhhhhhhhhhhh

Jonnie: I hate Knecht Ruprecht

Sandra: his book says "Strafregister" - that means "index of punishments"

Jonnie: AAAAHAHA!

Jonnie: so they come by on the 6th??

Sandra: they have nothing to do with Christmas

Jonnie: So who comes on Christmas again?

Sandra: the christkind

Sandra: the christkind is a sweet little angle or so

Sandra: the Santa Claus you have in America was invented by Coca Cola, I think

American kids are so spoiled.

(Source: I'm Nacho Steppinstone - November 20, 2004)

Unsung Heroes

Bearded John - Valdez, Alaska – Summer, 1991:

In order to raise beer money, Bearded John buried himself in fish heads & charged people $1 to take a picture.

(Source: I'm Nacho Steppinstone – January 12, 2004)

Crisis-Line

Last night, Belle was being a criminal mastermind like usual. She faked an emotional crisis while we were chatting on I.M. (with no apparent motivation, aside from her own amusement). This fiasco provided me with a rare opportunity for exercising my crisis prevention skills since it was not clear she was pulling my leg.

I'm glad she was faking her crises, because my counseling skills are piss-poor. At one point when she was hysterically describing an uncle who had given her the "bad touch", my response was, "It is not *bad*. It is *controversial*".

The best advice I could think of was, "You should eat a cookie"! And, "Find somebody who can give you a piggyback ride! A piggyback ride will take care of everything"!

So, yeah, it's good I don't work at a crisis prevention line. I don't think I'd hold that job very long.

Commentary –

More of the Pearls of Wisdom Jonnie offered me during my fake emotional crisis were to, "Eat some cereal" and to "Call the Mayor".

I'm sorry I'm so evil, Jonnie, but I laughed so hard last night I think I peed a little.

- Belle

Maybe your emotional radar is so finely tuned you knew it was a fakeout. Deep down. You knew.

- AmyJo

I *did* know on a subconscious level. Because Belle *lies* constantly.

- Jonnie

(Source: I'm Nacho Steppinstone – June 16, 2004)

Three Cool Things About My Mechanic

1. When I was working in the gas station, he asked me one day, "You ever get into my tools"? I thought he was accusing me of stealing something and told him I don't give a shit about his tools. He then gestured to a big red metal chest and said, "Look in there". I did and it was full of porn! His final word on the matter was, "Don't be in here jacking off when customers are around".

2. He changed a fuel filter for one of the shop's clerks, who couldn't figure out how to do it himself. He also cut the bottom out of the old metal filter and hung a nut in there, making a little bell which he then attached to the bottom of the guy's car. The next day the guy came into the shop in a panic, "Whenever I turn, there's a 'clang clang clang' underneath my car". He was almost crying. Ron fixed the problem, but not being crooked, didn't charge the guy.

3. He carved a huge dick out of wood, sanded it until it was perfectly smooth, varnished it so it was all shiny, & made it into a screwdriver handle.

(Source: I'm Nacho Steppinstone – December 25, 2003)

Black Carlos Was Right

Some time back, a day-laborer I worked with ("Black Carlos") directed my attention to a chinese place located right in the center of my stomping grounds. It's a little hole in the wall place and I barely even noticed it before. It's so innocuous, that the neighboring donut shop steals the attention of a casual observer.

But anyway, Black Carlos told me they give you a TON of food for under $5.00. I wasn't sure if he was full of shit or not, but I tried it out a couple of weeks ago and he was right on the money! They give you a TON of food! You can barely close the lid on the takeout container. And it's, like, $4.85 or something like that. I always get a little change froma $5 bill.

So, all his other bullshit aside, Black Carlos was right. The other thing he told me was "that degree will get you a job". Then whenever I tried to comment, he would cut me off - "You get that degree! That degree will get you a job!! They'll say, 'Well, he got that degree, he must know somethin'!'" We'll see how that theory works out.

He also said, "Jonnie, you're a beautiful person. I really mean that. On the inside, I mean" (he said that after I gave him a ride to the liquor store after work). He paid me a little gas money too, so I said "thanks" (In retrospect, I wish I'd have said, "Black Carlos, you are beautiful too" when he gave me gas money because a lot of guys don't pay for gas).

hmmm...what else did he say?

He said a lot of shit.

We were working on a construction site and he goes, "All this work just so some rich white guy can move in"! Then there was an awkward silence since I am a white guy (though a broke one). Then I replied with something like, "Well...what have rich white guys ever done for me?" [answer – Nothing] because it really was more of a class issue than a race issue - and then everything was back to normal again.

(Source: Rebel Leady Boy – March 03, 2006)

True Security Guard Fantasies

In the late 1980s, I had a 3rd-shift security guard job in a factory from about 11:00 in the evening until 7:00 in the morning.

There really weren't too many responsibilities. They just paid a guard at night to make patrols and to keep their insurance costs down. I liked it because I could study while I was on the clock.

But I only bring it up because I remembered another guard there named Werner. He was one of those fat-ass wannabe cops who thinks a security guard job is the same thing as joining a S.W.A.T. team or something.

Anyway, I only bring up Werner because of his fucked up fantasy life.

Tonight at work, I recalled one particular evening's shift change when he started rambling on and on about how he'd love for somebody to try to break into his house so he could shoot them legally and how if they weren't armed, he would put another gun in their hand to justify the shooting. And he was just going on and on about it.
Eventually, he drew me a diagram of his fantasy home which included a large pyramid structure with a hot tub at the top.
The sides of the pyramids were made up of stairs, like this:

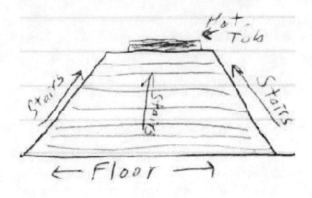

Jonnie's recreation of Werner's fantasy love-spa.

As if that weren't ridiculous enough, he discussed how he could be up there with his wife and the pyramid base would be high enough that he could see the entire surrounding area from the comfort of his hot tub and nobody could ever sneak up on him.

Then he went on to describe a detailed fantasy in which he is in the hot tub with his wife (with a bunch of guns in close proximity, just in case he needs them) and he notices somebody trying to sneak up the pyramid. He said he would climb out of the hot tub, ask his wife to tie a towel around his exposed privates and then just flat out shoot the guy.

As the fantasy progresses, he notices people coming up on all sides of the pyramid and starts blowing them all away as his wife keeps passing him fresh ammo.

?????
What kind of a retarded fantasy is that???

He also was 100% POSITIVE that he could write an amazing screenplay based around that scenario. He just KNEW it in his SOUL.

hahaha - poor stupid Werner.

Comments –

HAHAHAHA.

To be honest - I think I would watch that movie.

- Sandra

(Source: Rebel Leady Boy – June 16, 2005)

Bluffton, Indiana – Jonnie's Birthplace and Gilliomville Headquarters.

Introducing:

Donald Kilbuck, Soul Saver

I will probably be at Dutch Harbor processing fish where the people will not be afraid of my straight forward threats that don't really mean anything.

- Donald Kilbuck

Introduction

I originally met Donald in a Valdez, Alaska fish processing camp, summer of 1991. He made a huge impression on me and we corresponded periodically over the years. When I returned to Alaska in 1994, we got back in touch and he acted as my traveling companion and general sidekick off and on throughout the rest of the '90s. Now in his 50s, Donald has lived his life as a perpetual transient. I've never seen him establish roots for more than a few months at a time. During my time in Alaska, Donald was always willing to drop everything and take a two or three day roadtrip on short notice and he constantly provided entertaining commentary on pretty much anything (favorite topics include his Alaska Native Corporation, former Alaska Governor Hickel, his girlfriend Lucy, professional wrestling, and John Lennon). Donald is the only person I've ever met who was willing to let me play Yoko Ono CDs in his van over and over for hours. I thought Donald warranted his own chapter.

Donald, James A., and Jonnie in Cordova, Alaska (June, 1991).

Xmas Cheer - For Free!

Some years back, Donald was working third shift in Anchorage. When he got off work early in the morning on "trash day" (the day when everybody has their garbage sitting outside), he would rummage through the neighborhood garbage, looking for items of value and would hoard them in his van.

Donald in Homer, Alaska.

One day I asked him what he was planning to do with all "that junk" and he responded, "I'm going to give it away for Christmas presents this year".

I didn't think he was serious but then in early December when I was complaining about Christmas shopping, Donald commented, "Mine is already done - for free! hahahaha...".

And sure enough, his friend William received a rusty axe head (with a piece of broken handle still intact) and somebody received an old pair of burnt barbecue tongs...and I don't remember what all.

(Source: I'm Nacho Steppinstone - October 22, 2004)

Kilbuckian Prophecy

Donald offers a prophetic glimpse into Alaska's future —

Alaska, One Hundred Years From Now

Just spoke to Eule Wise-owl and he said cutting wood will be a thing of the past. Some kid said that cars will run on fish guts. Eskimo population will be 1 billion. Alaska will be it's own country. No more segregation. Palm trees, will grow, hot all year. Smoked fish will be enjoyed, whales will land on the beach and die, so we can cut the meat up and enjoy the meal raw hide. There will be lots of stealing. No form of government. Pot will grow with bounty.

And if that doesn't get your blood flowing, I've also posted screen captures from Today's Episode of *Soul Train.*

Get On Board!

(Source: I'm Nacho Steppinstone - January 29, 2005)

Porcupine Quills

According to Donald, Yu'pik craft shops sometimes will buy porcupine quills for use in manufacturing traditional Eskimo jewelry,.

Instead trapping or shooting the porcupine, I always thought Donald had a very clever and humane method for harvesting porcupine quills. He always had a couple of spare blankets in his vehicle, then if he saw a porcupine on the roadside, he could pull over and throw a blanket over it. By the time the porcupine freed itself, the blanket was full of quills and Donald could go cash them in.

(Source: I'm Nacho Steppinstone - December 15, 2004)

From Another Mother

Donald with a granola bar on the Cordova Ferry - circa 1991.

Selected Correspondance from Donald Wy. Kilbuck

(arranged more or less alphabetically) -

- "A kid was push brooming the cement parking lot, and it was blowing in the wind back at him there must be child labor law for that, would you look into that?"
- "Alaska is now really in cold weather 160 mile per second freezing white foxes, and polar bears that like to eat a great deal of warm meat."
- "A poltergeist took control...when i sat down in the restroom then pulled the empty coffee can over my mouth and shit at the same time then i got...hot flashes and different visions."
- "Are you having bad weather like most of the stormy California bad dreams? The palmtrees still stand? It's not the end?"

- "Candle light, star light, moon light, cat eyes, in the dark of night reading stories of wildlife running around with no where to roam, just in circles, circles of hope, with no rope to climb out of the dark what to do? It's raining here in Anchorage, Alaska and all of you are invited to burn at Willow, Alaska."
- "Charlies Angels is on the tube, my kind of Karate kicks, and stances...all their emotions w/ feelings that move my eye. Stand up hair!"
- "Chicken Legs, instant rice, broiled, and cooked! Gas is up again."
- "Crack it up! Bro! from another mother. Makes me think."
- "Donald Kilbuck @ shine on, rain on, off on, on again .com"
- "Early in the morning! Got to find another lover."
- "Earthquake in Alaska was a thrill with sway...it done some highway damage and created some labor for some people that needed that extra ca$h."
- "Emotional aches and pains go away...and the hair do is still in a form of no return".
- "Folk music is good! Just that you don't want to be caught dancing to a tune full of tears and shit that makes people think they stink!"
- "For anger management i made a pitstop at the Native Assembly of God Church to help move things around...Thats therapy for the thoughts. Scattered thoughts maybe, but it helps to move the thoughts around [wherever] they may land. A good sneeze helps the thoughts move too."
- "Get a job that will make your account balance like sweet potato."
- "God help us all i am not all here. This must be another hell hole that God made for all the bad people too enjoy. Lot of nuts at work".
- "God she is a dingbat, but i like dingbats sometimes. Long as they don't bother me for a hand out, or bother me where their keys are".
- "Ha! All the world is in such a mess.
  Makes my weather up here normal."
- "Hi! Kodiak is having a very sunny day! And the wind is against my face when i ride down hills around here so flies smash into me too. Hahaha!"

- "Hurry up and get up here with all the tools that you can find along the way".
- "I am going towards the fishing hole that is on Holy Grounds...So I guess that will be another experience w/ fishing and clouds. Dance with my shadow."
- "I am harvesting all the ocean's flavors".
- "I am now seeking a place to put down my hat of many colors."
- "I am so bored that i want to see a barber".
- "I am swinging around Kodiak, Alaska. Air is fine! The rain is also fine. no work, butt that is also fine".
- "I am totally smelling the ink off the all American Currency right now. I didn't go to work again although i really don't miss the hard labor. The fun part i miss."
- "I could free all the animals when i get excited but i would have to have all professional crew. Not no scary alcoholicks running loose like rabbits hopping."
- "I don't attend the messages and songs God has for me too hear."
- "I drank sleepy time tea, doesn't seem to work though. Maybe that pill the doctor told me not to drive with will work."
- "i got fired at the Commons Building...And i wasn't smiling. Now i am looking for a full time work...Maybe i am best when i am not sweating."
- "I got my oil changed and brakes checked. Gas filled and now i am ready to chase the moon."
- "I guess in order to swim in this world we got to take care of our best beastly body".
- "I hope I make it to 59...I have a new Dr. that I really like and trust...He did say he believed my life expectancy could be well into the 70's. You see why I like him?"
- "I looked @ pictures of babies too on the wall with all kinds of smiles...babies that made the world sing out loud and then some"
- "I love to pee into the wind so the perfect hairstyle can have a smell to it. "
- "I SEEN SOME WILD BIRD THAT NEEDED TO BE BLOW DARTED AT OR BOW N ARROW, BUT NOTHING AT HAND OR ANY CAMERA TO SHOOT THE FEATHERED FEAST. I AM COMING DOWN WITH A COLD OR WHATEVER IT IS".

- "I shall get a hold of my emotions and scatter the thoughts."
- "I still have my short hairstyle that makes me look like i need a make over."
- "Is your asparagus out? Do you get the drift?"
- "I went to bingo for all the lost bingo players. Didn't win."
- "I will paint All the paint that needs to be placed on each wall or parts of the walls."
- "I've got sunshine!...with all the flavor of garlic and eggs."
- "I wonder how the plants will do if i leave them overnight in the garage guess i just have to find out."
- "Jay Leno is a wild man. I could party with that man."
- "Just clipped my hair down to the skinhead, and i feel fine."
- "Lastnight i watched my boss Fred, mop my floor that i rushed mop."
- "Let it be. Like a butterfly! Iron Butterfly...Hashish!"
- "Maybe i should get home. Or make my rounds, look square."
- "Might hunt wild feather birds for lunch."
- "Muscle spasm attack was very differant for my experience and all the doctor did was give me relaxer pills with x-ray vision".
- "now i want to wash and wax my Hemi Dodge Truck with all it's meaning."
- "Okay take care and tell everyone i says hell-o! And that the place here is not all here."
- "Raked in ca$h for singing from a tip jar. Cool!"
- "Silver Dollars are swimming in the tank."
- "SLEEP is good! I best make some caffeine go down. And look around my scattered room."
- "Sunshine is breaking through the cloud. So the plants will have some heat."
- "The Beatles is my favorite singers and personalities that arrived while i was starting to notice and hear music at 6th grade before Tex Ritter entertained me at a small Quatiant Hut. Everybody must rock!"
- "The ole farts were talking the fish stories...Some fisherman overflowed his wader and fell in. I did not laugh, for i got overflowed with my waders too."

- "The plants got watered...I watered the flowers w/ all i could. Then the trees of all kinds. The trash and litter from all the nerds, and weird looking people of all kinds."
- "There is a fish near a pineapple tree under the sea!"
- "THERE WILL BE DANCING AND DRUNK DRUMS! LOTS OF MONEY"
- "Today i clicked on Sandra for the first time and appeared to travel into pictures that i was amazed and i laughed"
- "Trying to call you is like trying to get into the Alaska Regional Medical Center on Sunday evening, the doors are all locked."
- "Weather is melting the winter ice, and snow from the roofs and it's really bright with the clear blue skies, with the mountains trying to hold on to the snow."
- "We keep trying to be busy. I am unloading and packing so i can unload and repack. It's like a merry go around up here or like the snow storms that we are having a stop and start affair with either love the snow or hate it. I got my snowshoes."
- "We seen a mother moose, and the baby was right behind her crossing the street. Then the squirrel was another wild animal seen on this beautiful day."
- "Wild feathers in the air! Rabbites with carrots. dirt roads, that are inviting under blue skies!"

(Source: personal and public correspondence from Donald Kilbuck)

When a Bear Awakes, What It Means to Hikers!

It usually means caution.
Or walk in groups or make noise when walking or biking.

I am enjoying my rain and wearing the $2.00 rain jacket from the thrift store that someone gave up or really didn't want it. It's a Coleman and it feels like a cheap sweat shop rain jacket from China. From China with LOVE! Anyways! I made a buy! Since Walmart sells their cheapies for 10 us dollars. Reading is good! Also walking backwards really slow and wide eyed! Not smelling like a guy that just drank a case of cheap beer. Amen! Smoking and smelling like smoked salmon is another.

(Source: Personal Communication – May 1, 2006)

DK On Unsavory Characters

Donald Kilbuck recently provided a fairly precise list of qualities he finds undesirable in a person:

> *One that puts extra details, is that one who overreacts to some small things, and makes problems bigger than it really is. One who is a bullshit, or has a chest that isn't really big. One big eyeballer. One who dyes hair that isn't real. One who farts silently.*

I think we can all relate.

(Source: Rebel Leady Boy - January 28, 2006)

Donald's Early Years.

Good Ideas

My desire is not all together cause the world is not round...the ships are catching a lot of fish that we can eat. Eat all you can!

- Donald Kilbuck

Testing

You're getting sleeeeeepyyyy....
Jonnie is HOT....
You want to give him pie and burritos and beer...
You won't remember reading this post...

(Did it work?)

(Source: I'm Nacho Steppinstone - November 05, 2004)

Toad Licking

I'm going to get a regular toad and charge club kids $5 to lick it.

Is there anything illegal about charging people to lick a non-hallucinogenic toad?

(Source: I'm Nacho Steppinstone - January 16, 2004)

Publicity Stunt

I am going to carve the Hulk out of a huge pickle.

Commentary -

Maybe the Hulk out of a cucumber and Bruce Banner out of a bratwurst

- Jonnie

(Source: I'm Nacho Steppinstone – February 06, 2005)

Schizo Coffee

I was working in a schizophrenic halfway-house for awhile. The residents had been released from the city mental institution and were placed in a block of apartments with an adjoining staff area so they could have their living skills evaluated before being set out into the community.

There was this guy, Ray, who constantly had his coffee maker on, he just refused to shut it off. Eventually, the coffee maker began to show signs of melt-down and was determined a fire hazard by the staff, so they removed it.

So anyway, I dropped by one day on my rounds and noticed Ray having a hot cup of coffee like usual.

Me: "Hey, they got you a new coffee maker"?

Ray: "Nah, I've been making it in the dishwasher".

Me: "?????????????"

I went over to the dishwasher, and sure enough, he was throwing in a bunch of coffee grounds instead of soap, running a cycle, then stopping it before the water drained out. The entire bottom of the dishwasher was full of hot coffee. Then it was just a matter of dipping a cup in there.

Resourceful guy, that Ray. He earned my respect that day.

Commentary –

Wow, that's like schizophrenic McGuyver!

- Gwen

Ray is a Gangsta!

- Muscle68

(Source: I'm Nacho Steppinstone - January 03, 2004)

Tattoo Idea

Brother Todd was telling me about a guy in Texas who had a tattoo of Jesus Christ on his chest and a woman on his back and he'd always tell people, "I've got Jesus in my heart and a bitch on my back". Then we must've talked about Superman tattoos too because I got confused and thought Todd was saying the guy had a tattoo of Jesus hanging on the cross with blood pooling up on his chest to form Superman's "S" logo.

That would be a badass tattoo.

Commentary –

Leave it to Jonnie to come up with some shit like that.

- Maxine

(Source: I'm Nacho Steppinstone - December 22, 2003)

Your Comments:

_____

_____

_____

Glue-All

I use a glue-like hair product which makes spikes that are not overly dry, hard, or shiny. It is almost exactly like glue in color and texture and I've noticed some of the larger hair product companies are begining to consciously refer to their similar (but inferior) products as "glue". They are also starting to incorporate glue-dispenser-esque packaging in some cases.

This phenomenon inspired me to transfer my hair product to a real glue bottle.

Secret hardcore hair goop dispenser.

It feels real hardcore to put glue in my hair every morning.

[**Postscript** – After I transferred my hair product to the glue bottle, I transferred the glue to a plastic baggy. In retrospect, I should've put the glue into the hair product dispenser and returned it to the store shelf as a prank. Instead, I put the bag of glue on the train tracks for part of my week-long series, "What Should I Put On the TrainTracks?", over at *The Real World…Blogger Style!*]

(Source: Rebel Leady Boy – December 17, 2005)

RLB's Time Saving Tips

RLB's Time Saving Tips will be a regular column in which Rebel Leady Boy relates practical advice about how to get the most from each day's 24 hour time limit.

Time Saving Tip #1 –

Clip your fingernails at work.

This will free up a little more liesure time later at home.

No need to thank me.

Commentary –

Thank you RLB! You make my life better.

- Sandra

I try to do what I can.
No need to pay me.

- Rebel Leady Boy

(Source: Rebel Leady Boy - February 26, 2006)

Perpetual Motion

Theoretically, it's possible to address a piece of mail so it floats perpetually through the system as long as a functional postal bureaucracy exists to forward it.

I'm thinking here of turning in a series of "Mail Forwarding" addresses linking a series of cities all over the country and then after 10 or so changes, the last one is forwarded to the first, making a "circle" with nobody ever actually receiving the package. I would like to do this with my ashes after death in order to replicate my experiences in life (circular and pointless meandering).

I'd also be willing to bet there are others out there who would pay for the service as an alternate to burial. I should approach people about that, maybe make a website & solicit customers.

Commentary –

You never know where the efficient postal workers are (and some do exist) so your ashes would probably wind up in the dead letter room which is semi-appropriate, eh?

- Kat

(Source: I'm Nacho Steppinstone - January 28, 2004)

Soul Food

Today, Sandra and I finally got out to Southern California's famous *Roscoe's House of Chicken & Waffles.*

Chicken & waffles really go together a lot better than you'd think.

Sandra had a quarter chicken with two waffles and I had the same, but with gravy over my chicken. We opted for breasts. Who wouldn't?

Yum!

(Source: Jonnie & Sandra – August 24, 2004)

What Do You Want?

Some recent search engine queries that brought visitors to *Rebel Leady Boy Scrapbook*:

- amish healthcare
- anchorage taco bell camera
- Bob Barker piggyback ride
- come mr tally man tally my banana
- dogs peeing on the wall
- funny cabbage
- great butt excercises
- hitler yelling

- how to be a fat sumo
- how to counterfit $20
- how does mass affect a pinewood derby car?
- i'm in jail
- incredible hulk nightlight
- jonnie esoteric
- old lady half werewolf
- pee in the coffee pot
- scrapbook boy
- supergirl porn
- testicle punishment
- what is the best outfit to wear for a singing competition

I know the disappointment which comes from clicking a search result only to find the linked site has nothing to do with what you were looking for. So I plan to start writing "wish fulfillment" posts based on search engine queries that mistakenly bring people here only to disappoint them.

Let the first one be "Bob Barker piggyback ride" –

Bob Barker Piggyback Ride.

So there's one visitor who should be 100% satisfied.

(Source: I'm Nacho Steppinstone – October 10, 2005)

Souvenirs & Ephemera

This one cabin was in the woods, dying from the ole age.

- Donald Kilbuck

Paging Mick Ulmer, Oriental Guide

In 1988, I attended the annual Tarzan Zerbini circus in Fort Wayne, Indiana. The Indiana Shriners hosted the event and photographs of their officers were included in the circus program.

As esoteric as they may appear, the Shriners were all pretty down to earth guys...not very mysterious or confounding at all. I hung around after the show and attempted to spot the Shriner officers depicted in my program and have them autograph their photos.

I did pretty well in a pretty short time because they were often congregating in small groups and if one agreed to sign, the others felt obligated to do likewise. So I would get two or three autographs at a time. The only autograph missing from my collection is Mick Ulmer, "Oriental Guide" –

MICK ULMER
Oriental Guide

So if anybody knows him, hook me up.

Commentary –

And they really DO look all mysterious and oriental!!! Absolutely NOT like average office guys only with stupid hats on, nooooo.

- Sandra

Hey, Jonnie- Mick Ulmer lives right here in Bluffton, Indiana. That is, he used to.

- Andi

WOW!!! I should've called him while I was down there!

Does he live in a castle?

- Jonnie

(Source: I'm Nacho Steppinstone – June 10, 2004)

Taco Bell Scrapbook

Here's a personal ad placed in a Valentine's Day edition of an Indiana newspaper, circa 1992. It is a message from "Larry" to "Laura Lynn".

Larry was apparently a Taco Bell employee and Laura Lynn was a customer.

Larry had at one point taken a photograph of Laura Lynn during one of her visits to his establishment & published it along with this message:

Laura Lynn,
You don't know me, but I love you.
I work at Taco Bell.
I was thinking maybe you love me too,
because you're there so much.
It's your smile I see when I melt the cheese on every Meximelt.
Please be mine.

Larry

haha

(Source: I'm Nacho Steppinstone - March 09, 2004)

On the Floor

One thing I've learned from hanging around with Donald Kilbuck is to look at the ground a lot because people are always dropping money. Donald has always had an uncanny knack for spotting lost money on the ground. I, on the other hand, rarely find money and I have not found *any* money on the ground at my current workplace. Not even once.

The sum of my loot so far amounts to —

1. A handwritten post-it note which reads:

A peacock feather adds elegance & pulls all the colors in this project together.

2. A mysterious drawing –

Any ideas?
It looks vaguely pornographic to me.

(Source: Rebel Leady Boy - March 21, 2006)

Your Comments:

The Muse Was Here

Let it never be said that Jonnie is not a writer.

I have already completed my first play –

Jonnie's One-Act Halloween Play.

I probably could have drawn it out a bit longer, but I think I've said all I have to say.

(Source: I'm Nacho Steppinstone - April 19, 2004)

Thou Shalt Not Croak

While discussing a website project, my client suddenly exclaimed, "Dude! You've *got* to meet *Moses*"!

I asked who Moses is and he is apparently a gritty biker turned bailbondsman/bounty hunter and he has a freaking steel CAGE built into the trunk of his car! For people!! Moses is a hard core mother fucker by all accounts.

But the best thing about Moses is his promotional t-shirt -

Moses' promotional t-shirt.

I just can't believe that shirt. The front reads, "Don't Go To Bed With A Price On Your Head" in an arresting yellow font while the main illustration incorporates the Biblical Moses mythos. Here, Moses the Bailbondsman parts a shark infested ocean so a ghettoed-out car can drive through to freedom. The caption reads, "When you're in deep water, call Moses".

I particularly like the dolphin lying in front of the car and the Ten Commandments tablet –

Thou shalt not croak

I'm impressed and amazed. Definitely call Moses if you ever find yourself in jail in Southern California.

Commentary –

Wow. I ... Wow.

- Zann

Moses is my dream guy.

- Belle

(Source: I'm Nacho Steppinstone - May 18, 2004)

FYI

While I was marking up old Gilliomville messageboard posts for a future XML search engine, I stumbled across this nugget from Brother Todd.

He located a "typology of homeless people" published in the 1920s which breaks them down into 3 catagories with distinct characteristics:

a *hobo* is a migratory worker
a *tramp* is a migratory non-worker
a *bum* is a non-migratory non-worker

A later study in 1993 identified further sub-types -

Redneck Bums drink a lot and they travel in packs and they like to fight.

Hippie Tramps do drugs and make money by selling drugs to college students.

So let's not generalize.

Commentary –

How about Supertramps?

- AmyJo

A Supertramp sells drugs to rock and roll bands.

- Jonnie

(Source: I'm Nacho Steppinstone - October 19, 2004)

Something You Don't See Everyday

Here's something you don't see everyday:

I encountered this memorial at an L.A. dogpark and the text reads:

In Memory of all Dogs Killed at Hiroshima and Nagasaki.

Nice gesture, I guess.

Commentary -

that picture makes me sad...it makes me profoundly sad.

- The Pimpress

(Source: I'm Nacho Steppinstone – December 14, 2003)

A Place to Store My Hulk Hands

[From when the RW...BSers were posting pictures of their bathrooms]

Note the ergonomic toilet plunger handle.

(Source: The Real World...Blogger Style! – March 10, 2004)

Your Comments:

_____

_____

_____

_____

_____

From Jonnie's Utility Belt

I call this the "tri-lighter" -

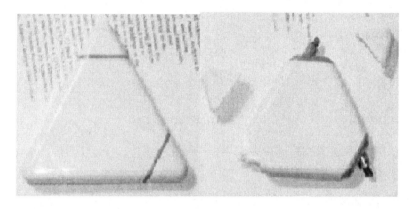

It's a 3-pronged, multi-colored highlighter.

The company that manufactures it provides "vital records" services, my two favorite of which are:

1. *Underground climate-controlled vaults* - For really important records. Built underneath a mountain in an undisclosed location, records stored in these vaults will reportedly survive a nuclear explosion.

Then, on the other end of the scale:

2. *Pulping services* - For extremely sensitive documents (when shredding is just not thorough enough). Documents are cross-cut shredded into confetti and then mixed with water (or a light acid) until they form an illegible gelatinous mass.

Confession - I've never actually used the tri-lighter.

I just keep it around to intimidate people.

Commentary -

What document could possibly be so important it would need to survive a nuclear attack?

- AmyJo

Probably documents showing that people owe you money, so you can still bill them after a nuclear explosion.

And definately any nuclear explosion insurance policies.

- Jonnie

(Source: Rebel Leady Boy – October 04, 2005)

My Linguistic Profile

80% General American English

15% Yankee

5% Upper Midwestern

0% Dixie

0% Midwestern

[From: http://www.blogthings.com/amenglishdialecttest]

Commentary –

I wondered about the "Pop" and "Soda" thing. I used to say "Pop" in the Midwest, then "Soda-Pop", now just "Soda".

I think pronouncing "caramel" as "carmel" is definitely a Midwestern regionalism though.

- Jonnie

If you're from the Midwest, you say pop but as you become more worldy you say soda.

Television has really done a lot to kill regional dialects. That's why the General American English percentages rank so high.

- Boz

I'm gonna start saying "Pop" again to represent my midwestern roots.

- Jonnie

In parts of New England they used to call soft drinks DOPE.

- Boz

(Source: The Real World...Blogger Style! – March 26, 2006)

Ephemera Deluxe

I don't know if anybody remembers WWF professional wrestling team *DX*, but *"Suck it!"* was one of their catch phrases.

DX was also the name of a Japanese (pain relief?) product.

I guess that's all the information you need to get this –

(Source: I'm Nacho Steppinstone - December 12, 2004)

From PVC

I received a great gift in the mail from Purple Viper today!

It's a collectible shower head from a 1980s line of novelty products called "Shower Heads". I think they were trying to say they put the "head" in "shower head" (or something like that) because they produced a whole series of shower heads adorned with rubber representations of various human and animal heads.

My shower head is particularly appropriate because it features former president Richard Nixon.

It easily replaced my old shower head and the results were glorious –

Thank you, Purple Viper!!
I owe you big-time, let me know if you ever need anything from California.

(Source: Rebel Leady Boy – October 24, 2005)

Self-Knowledge

I just ran "jonnie" through the *Googlism* [**www.googlism.com**] site and learned quite a bit about myself –

jonnie is doing fine and we believe there is a cure for leukemia

jonnie is very sleepy from his sedation

jonnie is een spin en iedereen is bang voor hem

jonnie is found to be unusually intelligent and is educated to speak and understand the aliens language

jonnie is the language of his race

jonnie is running in slow motion with concrete shattering around him in gunfire

jonnie is thrown into a cage and brought to denver

jonnie is using his time to obtain weapons including jets and an atomic bomb to lead a revolt

jonnie is an utter dumb ass

jonnie is about to turn the tables

jonnie is a large door with big fuckin metal shafts across it

jonnie is a member of the remaining tribes of cave

jonnie is one of the quietest and most well mannered young men you are ever likely to meet

jonnie is a 5

(Source: I'm Nacho Steppinstone – June 14, 2004)

An After-Word

By Jon David

Well, there you have it. The small exemplification of that which is the life and times thus far of the man and those around Jonnie Gilliom—Jonnie 7-11—Nacho Steppinstone—Rebel Leady Boy. The every-day life of the man whose days are not unlike those of every-life, but more satisfactory when the absurdity of that life's days is recognized.

On an everyman afternoon in every-day high school in 1988, long before the internet or blogging hit any of our lives, when people put their most mundanely absurd thoughts in diaries that were then put in their top drawer before going to bed at night rather than posted for the world to think about and when something funny or awkward could only be circulated to the people that you saw in the days following, I stood laughing myself into hysterics in the corner of the boys' restroom in our school in Northeast Indiana as I witnessed the impromptu Opera mentioned in the Introduction. I heard the King of the Urinal—Jonnie—call out for the audience to "hear my flush, fear my flush" as he struck the handle of the urinal to an orchestrated flash, while his confederate Duane sang response as the Queen of the Stall.

It was a shining moment of nonsense that makes me laugh every time it revisits, and one that would be lost but for the memory and rumor of the few there and those that heard about it in bars afterward. The Opera was a spontaneous tick. Jonnie's collection grabs moments like that and serves the dual purpose of memorializing them and sharing them with pretty much anyone that is willing to take the time to read about it.

Each account in Content will revisit you long after the reading while you sit in a quiet office or in the solitude of a bus during your evening commute when you have a moment to yourself to remember them. And they will make you happy.